DESTINY INK

Talent Show Magic

nosy crow

First published in the UK in 2024 by Nosy Crow Ltd
Wheat Wharf, 27a Shad Thames,
London, SE1 2XZ, UK

Nosy Crow Eireann Ltd
44 Orchard Grove, Kenmare,
Co Kerry, V93 FY22, Ireland

Nosy Crow and associated logos are trademarks and/or registered
trademarks of Nosy Crow Ltd.

Text and illustrations copyright © Storymix Limited 2024
Written and illustrated by Adeola Sokunbi

The right of Adeola Sokunbi to be identified as the
author and illustrator of this work has been asserted.

ISBN: 978 1 80513 234 9

A CIP catalogue record for this book is available from the British Library.

Printed and bound in Great Britain by Clays Ltd, Elcograf S.p.A.
following rigorous ethical sourcing standards.

MIX
Paper | Supporting
responsible forestry
FSC® C018072

1 3 5 7 9 10 8 6 4 2

www.nosycrow.com

To D.B.,
my book buddy ♡

A.S.

This is me,
DESTINY INK.

I love drawing and doodling. I can't wait for you to come on an adventure with me!

This is
FUZZY,
my pet hamster.
Isn't he the cutest?

This is my **MUM** and **DAD**.

They're the greatest!

This is **GRANNY GAIL**. →

She's helping me get ready to perform in a talent show. Turn over and find out what happens!

CHAPTER ONE

I've been practising magic tricks all day, with Fuzzy. He's my hamster but he makes a pretty good magician's assistant too.

We're really **EXCITED** because we're performing at the

community talent show tomorrow. Anyone can perform at the talent show. My granny Gail is helping to organise it.

There's going to be a lantern parade, food and drink stalls, fireworks and even a light show! (I've never seen one before but Granny Gail told me there'll be lots of cool lasers.)

My favourite trick is when
I pull Fuzzy out of my hat.

"TA-DAAAAAA!"

"Nice work, Fuzzy," I say. "Then
at the end of our act, we'll take a
bow, like this."

"Don't worry, Fuzzy. We have
time to practise your bow – you're
going to be great, trust me!"

We've only ever performed
our magic tricks for family and
never on a stage before, but I've
learned it's good to try new

things. The other day, I had a
SLEEPOVER outside for
the first time! It was at my
best friend Olivia's house
and was completely brilliant.
I had been worried about
it at first, but I gave it
a try and it turned
out I loved it.

It was totally **INKTASTIC**.

Inktastic is my catchphrase, by the way. It's a mash-up of my two favourite words: *fantastic*, and my surname, *Ink*. Do you get it?

INKTASTIC!

"Hmmm, what trick should we practise next?" I ask. I pull the items from my bag of magic tricks and lay them on the table.

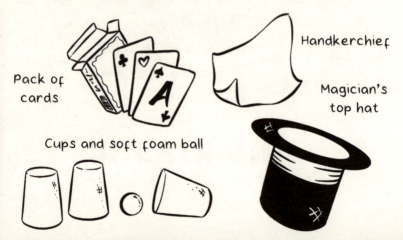

Pack of cards

Handkerchief

Magician's top hat

Cups and soft foam ball

DIIIING-DOOOOONG.

"Granny Gail is here!" Mum says. I drop my cards and run to the door.

Granny Gail is coming over to help make my magician's cape for the performance. She's really good at making things. She can sew, knit AND paint.

I open the door and we do our secret handshake.

"I found some gorgeous fabric for your magician's cape at the market this morning," says Granny Gail. She pulls out a huge wad of purple velvet fabric from her bag.

"I love it!" I say, stroking the soft material. It feels like just the sort of thing a real magician would wear.

Granny Gail smiles as she takes off her shoes. I follow her into the kitchen, where Dad is bustling around with the pots and pans.

"Hello, son," Granny Gail says. She hands Dad three plantains from her bag. "I got these for you too."

"Thanks, Mum!"

Granny Gail flips on the kettle, then makes herself comfortable. She rummages through her bag again and this time she brings out a whole heap of

BITS AND BOBS.

Fabric glue

Old yellow T-shirt

Measuring tape

Sewing needle and thread

Box of pins

Chalk

Scissors

GLUE

PINS

Dad brings over a plate of fruit and biscuits and juice for me, and peppermint tea for Granny Gail. "Some snacks and drinks to keep your strength up – making things is hard work!"

I grab my **INKTASTIC** sketchbook and pen and show Granny Gail the designs I've drawn for the cape. We choose our favourite and get to work.

my fave

Granny Gail gets me to stand
with my arms out to my sides.
She pulls a measuring tape and
a piece of chalk from her pocket,
then holds the purple
fabric up to my body.

Granny Gail shuffles
around, taking
measurements
here and there -
drawing lines
on the cloth.

Next, she uses
the scissors to cut along
the lines that she drew on the
fabric. Then she folds the edges
in, holding them down with the pins.

Finally, she gets to work with the sewing needle and thread, making neat stitches along the folds.

I cut lots of big stars out of the old T-shirt, which Granny Gail then stitches on to the cape. She holds the finished cape up.

"TA-DAAA!"

"Thanks, GG, it's **INKTASTIC**," I say. "Now we need an outfit for Fuzzy!"

Granny Gail and me make a teeny-tiny, very fancy headdress for Fuzzy.

I put my cape on
and spin around.
It billows out
behind me.
I look like a
proper magician now.

"What will your stage name be,
Destiny?" asks Dad. "How about
THE GREAT DESTINY INK?"
"Or, how about **MARVELLOUS
DESTINY INK**?" suggests
Granny Gail.

I think very hard.

"I've got something even better," I say at last, leaping out of my chair. "Ladies and gentlemen, I am

THE GREAT
INKTASTIC
DESTINY INK

and this is my glamorous

assistant,

THE MAGNIFICENT

FUZZY!"

Fuzzy and I want the magic show to be **PERFECT** so we spend the rest of the day practising our tricks over and over again.

I use my speedy card-shuffling skills and **WOW** Granny Gail with a card trick.

Is **THIS** your card?

Then I **AMAZE** Mum and Dad by performing my ball and cup trick.

After dinner, we video call my cousins and I show them the magic trick where I pull Fuzzy out of my magician's hat. They clap and **CHEER** for me. It feels so good!

At bedtime, Dad drives Granny Gail home.

"I can't wait for the dress rehearsal tomorrow," I say to Fuzzy as we snuggle down in bed. "I hope the crowd enjoys our magic tricks."

I yawn and imagine wowing everyone with our act.

"Maybe I should be a famous magician full-time. What do you think, Fuzzy?" I look over to him, but he's already snoring. I drift off to sleep dreaming of applause.

CHAPTER TWO

The next morning, Granny Gail and I arrive at our local park for the dress rehearsal. Fuzzy pokes his head out of my pocket and I help to straighten his headdress. My new cape billows out behind me as

we walk through the park gates.
Fuzzy and I look around in awe.

Paper lanterns of different
shapes, sizes and colours line
the stone path in front of us.

People are busy setting up
food and drink stalls, and hanging
fairy lights in the trees all around
the park.

We walk along the path towards a big stage where a man wearing a pair of headphones is fiddling around with a microphone. He's a lot bigger than me, but even he looks tiny up on the stage. I hold on to my bag of tricks tightly.

"Testing, testing, one two three." The muffled voice of the man onstage pierces through the park, followed by a loud

SCREEEEECH.

I wince and cover Fuzzy's ears – he doesn't like loud noises.

"At least people will know where the stage is," mumbles Granny Gail, removing her hands from her own ears.

When we reach the stage, people are putting out rows of chairs and there are also blankets for even more people to sit on at the very front. My tummy starts to feel heavy, like someone dropped a big rock inside it. There'll be a lot of people watching the magic show - way more than I imagined.

I swallow hard. **GULP!** This is going to feel very different to performing at home...

"Gail, you're here at last!"

A lady with a red sparkly dress is walking towards us.

"Oh, shush, you," Granny Gail laughs. "Delia, please let me introduce

THE GREAT INKTASTIC DESTINY INK!"

I clear my throat. "Ahem - and this is **THE MAGNIFICENT FUZZY**, my assistant." Fuzzy does his pose for Delia and Granny Gail.

"Oh, Destiny! You look amazing! It's great that you'll have a friend up onstage with you," says Delia. "I wish Gail was singing with me." Delia looks hard at Granny Gail with her eyebrow raised like this.

Delia puts her arm around Granny Gail. "Your gran's got a brilliant voice, you know."

"Delia, you know performing

onstage isn't for me," says Granny Gail. "I'm more than happy to sing in front of friends and family, but on a **BIG** stage like this one? No thanks!"

Delia sighs. "OK, well, for now I'll just be thankful for this wonderful dress that you made me." Delia twirls around. "Did your gran ever tell you what a talented seamstress she is, Destiny?"

"Oh, I know." I give a twirl of my own. "She made **MY** cape too!"

The man onstage asks for the performers to take their places for the dress rehearsal. Some of the people who were setting up the stalls and hanging the lights, make their way over to watch.

Granny Gail gives me a kiss. "I'll be sitting in the audience," she says. "Right in the front, where you can see me."

Suddenly my mouth has gone very dry, like a desert.

WATER...

"You'll **SMASH** it, Destiny!"
Granny Gail says, taking her seat.

I nod and give Granny Gail a
shaky smile. It feels like I'm
walking in sticky mud and with
each step towards the stage,
I sink deeper into it.

"The stage
really is
big, isn't
it?" I say
to Fuzzy.
His whiskers
droop, which
means he's
feeling
nervous.

NERVOUS   SCARED

HAPPY   SUPER HAPPY

The first act to go onstage is a group of teenagers in baggy trousers and matching hats. Loud, upbeat music starts to play and they break out into an energetic dance with loads of flips and tricks. One of them even spins upside down on his head!

My mouth is **WIDE OPEN** with amazement by the time they finish. The other acts and I cheer and clap as they bound off the stage with huge smiles.

"Next up, Helena Hula Hoop!"

A tall girl in a shiny costume and leggings, with a huge stack of multicoloured hula hoops, steps on to the stage.

She starts her act by spinning one hula hoop around her waist while the rest lie beside her on the floor. And then she uses one foot to scoop up another hoop from the floor. She tosses it smoothly over her head, so she's now spinning two. Then she does it again and again, until she's spinning **TWENTY HULA HOOPS** at the same time!

She moves her arms and legs,
creating amazing shapes, and the
whole time the
hoops never
stop spinning.

The fun
performance
ends with her
tossing the
hoops through
the air to land
around a glittery pole on the
other side of the stage.

The audience **WHOOP** and
cheer as she takes a bow.

"I think you would be good
at hula-hooping," I say to Fuzzy.

Delia is next up. She sweeps up on to the stage gracefully and a woman with a guitar joins her. She strums a few notes and then Delia begins singing. They start off slow, but the song gets faster and faster and Delia begins to clap her hands and stamp her feet to the beat of the song.

It's so cheerful and catchy that by the end of it, all the other performers are singing and clapping along. Delia gives a little curtsy and Granny Gail cheers extra loud from the audience.

"You're up next, Destiny," says Delia as she sweeps offstage.

But my legs feel heavy, like I'm **GLUED** to the ground.

I take one wobbly step forwards, and another, and another, until I'm standing in the middle of the huge empty stage.

Two helpers bring a table and place it in front of me. I set my bag of magic tricks down and look

out to the audience. Granny Gail
gives me a big thumbs up.

"I am **THE**

GREAT–"

The words come out as
one massive croak. Why
do I sound like a frog?!

I clear my throat, take a deep breath and try again. "I am

THE GREAT INKTASTIC DESTINY INK!"

and today I will be performing some real magic with the help of my assistant - **THE MAGNIFICENT FUZZY**."

Right on cue, Fuzzy jumps out from my pocket. His headdress is all wonky so I try to straighten it, but then I accidentally knock my bag of tricks off the table. I bend down to pick them up.

34

"Ahem," I say, standing up and putting the bag on the table. "My first trick will truly **AMAZE** you."

I reach for my magician's hat but it's not on my head! I must have left it backstage. I can't pull Fuzzy out of a hat without an actual hat.

I take a step back to go and fetch it, but I tread on my cape. I stumble backwards ... and then I trip over, landing on my bottom.

"You're OK, Destiny," calls Delia from the wings. "Keep going!"

I stumble to my feet. My face feels very hot. I take my cup and ball out of my bag and place them on the table. I show the ball to the audience. Then I place the ball under one of the cups.

I try to shuffle the cups around, just like I've done before, but this time it feels as though I'm trying to do the trick wearing big woollen mittens!

One of the cups flies off the edge of the table and the ball rolls out, bounces a few times and then falls off the stage.

My trick is ruined. Fuzzy looks up at me with his drooping whiskers. He looks like he might cry.

I grab Fuzzy and together we turn around and **RUN** off the stage, my magician's cape billowing out behind me.

CHAPTER THREE

Granny Gail finds me backstage
and pulls me into a huge Granny
Gail hug.

"I forgot my hat," I say sadly.
"And then I tripped on my cape
and then my ball and cup trick

didn't work... **EVERYTHING** went wrong!"

Granny Gail hugs me even tighter. "It sounds like you've got a case of the nerves, Destiny. It's normal to be nervous. It happens to all of us sometimes."

"Maybe I'll stick to performing just for family," I say. "I don't think Fuzzy and me want to be in the talent show after all."

39

The heavy feeling inside my tummy gets worse.

Granny Gail looks at me very carefully. "Let's not make a decision right now. Why don't we leave your name on the list and see how you feel later on? If you really don't want to perform, you don't have to."

"Ok." I nod. But deep down I'm thinking that Fuzzy and I should skip the talent show altogether.

When Granny Gail drops me home, a little bowl of chopped-up mango is waiting for me, and Mum is excited to hear all about the dress rehearsal.

"So, how did it go?" she asks as she sips her coffee.

My shoulders hunch over and I stare at my bowl. "All the other acts were **SO GOOD**. But when it was my turn, my throat went funny and then I messed up all my tricks ... and then I ran offstage."

"Oh, Destiny!" Mum says. "Don't get too down on yourself. I remember when I had to dance for a school show once. I was so nervous that I couldn't stop shaking!

But the buzz I got once it was over and everyone was clapping and cheering for me felt amazing. I can still feel it now." Mum smiles and looks off into the distance.

"How did you get over the nerves though, Mum?"

Mum thinks for a moment. "Well, some people say that imagining the audience in their underwear works for them."

"That sounds silly," I say.

"Yeah, that never worked for me either," says Mum. "When I get nervous, I close my eyes, and

42

I take a deep breath, then count to three. And then I slowly let my breath out and count to three again. And then I wiggle my arms really hard to shake all the nerves away."

I'm doing Mum's breathing trick and shaking my arms when I get a brainwave. I know something that *always* makes me feel better.

"I'm going to do some drawing," I say.

I run up to my bedroom and grab my sketchbook and pen, while Fuzzy has a lie-down.

I draw myself as **THE GREAT INKTASTIC DESTINY INK** - who is definitely *not* shy or nervous. I draw my cape and top hat and then I add a special magic wand. It can do real magic, of course, so I never have to worry about any of my tricks going wrong.

My wand can:

Fix
broken
pencils

Make things levitate

Find lost toys

Make me
teleport

"If I had a *real* magic wand
I wouldn't feel shy about
performing because my magic
would be out of this world!"

I swish my cape around, imagining that I am a famous magician.

I was right, I do feel a bit better. Maybe I'll practise the cup and ball trick again. I rummage around in my bag of tricks, but instead of my cup and ball, I pull out a magic wand! It's smooth and black, with a white strip at the top and the bottom. It looks just like the one I drew in my sketchbook.

"Hmm, I wonder..."

I strike a pose, imagining an audience in front of me.

I wave my wand towards Fuzzy.

ABRACADABRA,
soon you will see,
Bring my **HAMSTER**
straight to me!"

Bright sparks burst from my
wand and Fuzzy's cage door snaps
open. I watch in amazement as
he floats out of his cage.
Fuzzy wakes up
looking very
confused.

Fuzzy flies all around the room, scrambling his little arms and legs in the air, before coming in to land on my shoulder.

My wand can do *real* magic!

CHAPTER FOUR

I look around my room and point
the wand at my toys:

"Abracadabra,

LEAP and **PRANCE**,

Make my toys and teddies

DANCE!"

For a moment nothing happens
and I wonder if I imagined Fuzzy
floating across my bedroom. But
then Gregg, my favourite teddy,
twitches. Then he gets up
on to his feet and stretches,
as if he's waking up from a
thousand-year sleep.

He breaks out into a dance around the room and each time he passes one of my other toys they wake up too, stretching and joining in. We do a big toy-conga around my bedroom.

I turn on some music on my tablet and we make a dance circle. Gregg does a backflip and then spins on his head, just like the teenagers from the dress rehearsal.

Even Fuzzy joins in!
Then it's my turn
and I'm flinging
myself
around,
dancing,
when **CRASH!**
I accidentally
knock my lamp
off my shelf.

"Destiny! What's all that racket about?!" calls Dad.

"Sorry!" I shout back. "Just practising my magic!"

"What should I try next?" I look at my bed and another idea pops into my head. I wave my wand:

"Is it **THERE** or is it **HERE?** Make my whole bed **DISAPPEAR!**"

With a flash of light my bed vanishes!

I don't fancy sleeping on the floor though, so I wave my wand around the bedroom again:

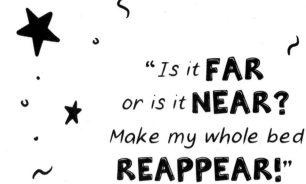

"*Is it* **FAR**
or is it **NEAR?**
Make my whole bed
REAPPEAR!"

There's another bright flash of light and my bed pops back with the pillows and duvet plopping down on top. This is so cool!

Now that I have *real* magic, there's no need to feel nervous about standing on that big stage - this is going to be the best magic show anyone has ever seen.

"Destiny, lunch is ready!" Dad calls from downstairs.

I skip to the kitchen with Fuzzy,

my magic wand safely tucked under my arm.

"You're looking much more bouncy than before. Feeling better now?" asks Dad.

I nod. "Yup. I found this magic wand in my room and I don't feel shy about performing in the talent show any more," I say. "I think I'm going to smash it, Dad!"

"That's great to hear." Dad puts a plate of fried rice and plantain and my cup on the table in front of me. He starts to walk towards the fridge when his phone rings.

"Could you make yourself a drink,

Destiny? I just need to answer this."

"No problem," I say, moving my eyebrows up and down at Fuzzy.

As soon as we're alone, I jump up on my chair and point my magic wand at the fridge.

" *Things go* **DOWN** *and things go* **UP**, **POUR** *my juice into my cup!*"

The fridge door snaps open, causing the bottles and jars inside to rattle and clang together.

The juice carton floats out of the fridge and across the room, just like Fuzzy did from his cage. The carton lid slowly turns, as if an invisible hand is unscrewing it.

Then the carton tips over, pouring the juice into my cup until it reaches the top. Then it drops on to the kitchen table, tipping on to its side and spilling orange juice everywhere.

"Oopsie." That was a bit messier than I had planned, but I can clean it up later. Now to make my drink a bit more special!

"**ABRACADABRA**,
delight and awe,
Give me a
VERY FANCY straw."

A curly-wurly straw with stripes and a big paper strawberry on top appears in the juice and I use it to take a sip.

"Mmm, refreshing," I say. I bet some ice would make this drink even better!

59

"*Abracadabra,*
COLD *and* **NICE**,
Add to my glass
some **CUBES OF ICE**."

An ice cube plops into my juice —
and then another, and another.

My wand gets wet, so I shake
the drops off and a bright flash
shoots from the tip of the wand
over to the spilled juice.

"UH-OH."

The spilled orange juice starts
to bubble and then whirl around
in a little whirlpool.

It wobbles across the table, soaking everything in sight. It knocks over my cup, splashes all over my plate of food and then heads straight for Fuzzy.

"Fuzzy, **WATCH OUT!**"

The whirlpool scoops up Fuzzy!

I grab my wand and wave it around.

"Whirlpool of juice,
we don't **WANT** to play
So we're asking you
to **GO AWAY!**"

The whirlpool begins to slow down until it splashes back down and then disappears altogether. My cup and plate of food clatter back down on to the tabletop, and I catch Fuzzy before he lands right on my rice. I quickly

grab the mop and a cloth out of the cupboard to wipe up the mess. I've only just sat down again when Dad comes back.

I try to do my 'I am totally innocent and haven't been getting up to magical mischief face'.

"Granny Gail's on her way over so we can all head off to the talent show together," he says. "How's the food?"

"It's awesome, Dad. Thanks!" I take another spoon of my orange-juice-flavoured rice.

When I've finished eating, I put my plate in the sink, pop my wand in my pocket and fetch my bag of magic tricks.

"How are you feeling about performing, Destiny?" asks Granny Gail. We're walking to the show with Mum and Dad following behind.

"**AMAZING**." I grin. "I found this magic wand, see?" I swish my wand around in front of Granny Gail. "I can do real magic now so I've got nothing to worry about."

I take my hat off and wave my magic wand:

"ABRACADABRA,
magic powers,
Give me a **PRETTY**
bunch of flowers."

I pull my hand out of the hat,
revealing a huge bunch of flowers.
I hand them to Granny Gail, and
she looks seriously impressed.

"Oh, wow. That's a new trick, Destiny. I'm so proud of you for giving performing another go."

When we get to the festival, the park looks magical. The lanterns are glowing and the fairy lights twinkle in the trees. Fuzzy and me sniff the air.

"DOUGHNUTS!"

"I'll buy us all doughnuts after the show!" Granny Gail says.

"You've got this, Destiny," says Mum once we get to the talent show stage. She gives me a kiss on the forehead. Dad sweeps me up into a big hug. "Show them how magnificent us Inks are," he says.

I nod confidently and stride backstage. When no one is looking, I magic up a cup of water. Being a magician is thirsty work.

I take a sip and place the cup next to my wand.

Fuzzy must be thirsty too. He leaps out of my pocket and balances on his back legs to take a few sips.

"Be careful, Fuzzy," I say.

Just then, the girl with the hula hoops comes offstage. As she swishes past, her hoops knock my wand off the table. And then someone else walks past and treads on it!

CRUNCH.

"Oh no, my wand!"

CHAPTER FIVE

I try to do some magic with
my wand, but nothing happens.
It's **BROKEN**.

"What happened to your wand,
Destiny?" asks Granny Gail, joining
me backstage.

"Someone trod on it. I can't do magic without it, so I can't go onstage!" I say.

"Well, that's not true," laughs Granny Gail. "I've watched you do magic tricks loads of times!"

"You don't understand..." I say.

"I know that performing in front of a crowd can feel scary, but I've been thinking – if my brave granddaughter can do it, I can do it too."

Granny Gail takes off her coat to reveal a beautiful sparkly dress.

It looks just like the one Delia was wearing.

SURPRISE!

"I was feeling nervous about singing onstage, but you've inspired me," says Granny Gail. "I've decided I'm going to perform with Delia onstage this evening."

I am seriously amazed. There's nothing Granny Gail can't do. I look down at my broken wand lying in my hands.

"I'm just not sure I can go onstage without my magic wand," I say sadly.

Granny Gail gives me a hug. "Oh, Destiny, you're **MAGIC** already. It's inside of you! It always has been. You don't need some magic wand to prove it – just be **YOU!**"

Right on cue, the presenter onstage makes an announcement. "Please put your hands together for the wonderful, the marvellous, Delia and Gail!" The crowd cheers as Granny Gail and Delia step out on to the stage.

I watch from the wings. Granny Gail seems a little stiff at first and she stumbles forward. I gasp. But once she's sung the first few lines, she seems to relax, and then Granny Gail really starts enjoying herself. Even Delia stands back, amazed, as Granny Gail sings and dances across the stage.

The crowd are on their feet, clapping and swaying. When they're done, the audience **ROARS** with cheers and applause.

I **WHOOP** and whistle from the wings. Fuzzy is jumping up and down with excitement too.

I look at my bag of magic tricks. I suppose it is possible to try the tricks I've been practising without my wand. I remember what Granny Gail said about me being magic with or without my wand.

"I need to show these people what us Inks can do!" I say to Fuzzy. "And if Granny Gail can do her thing onstage, then maybe I can too!"

"Next up:

THE GREAT INKTASTIC DESTINY INK!"

All of a sudden, my mouth goes dry and my heart starts beating really loudly in my chest. I close my eyes and take a deep breath, counting to three in my head. And then I let the breath out and count to three again.

1 ... 2 ... 3

Fuzzy climbs on to my shoulder,
giving his best magician's
assistant pose.

I walk out on to the stage.

"L-ladies and gentlemen." My
words come out as a squeak. I
clear my throat and start again.

"Ladies and gentlemen. I am

THE GREAT INKTASTIC
DESTINY INK

and this is my trusty assistant,

THE MAGNIFICENT
FUZZY.

Tonight we'll be showing you some
magic tricks!"

I start off with the cup and
ball trick, imagining that I'm
performing it at home just for
Mum and Dad. The crowd **OOHS**
and **AAHS** and they clap when
I finish. We're off to a good start.

My throat isn't feeling dry any more, so when I announce my next trick, my words come out loud and clear.

I flip and shuffle my cards the way I did yesterday when I showed Granny Gail. I finish with a flourish and the applause is even louder!

By the time I pull Fuzzy from my hat for the finale, I'm buzzing. Fuzzy strikes the most **INKTASTIC** magician's assistant pose he's ever done and the crowd go **WILD**. Mum and Dad stand up and everyone joins them, cheering. It's a standing ovation!

CHAPTER SIX

Fuzzy and I watch the rest of the show from the wings. There's a steel band and an awesome gymnastics act. We cheer until my throat feels tickly.

After the show, all of the

performers are celebrating
backstage.

"Well done, Destiny! You were
amazing!" says Granny Gail.

"You were
too!" I grin.

Mum and
Dad come
rushing over.

"You were
wonderful,
Destiny!"
says Mum.

"I think that
was your best
performance
yet!" says Dad.

Granny Gail buys me a doughnut
and it tastes amazing!

Dad buys us all some patties and he gives Fuzzy some carrots that we brought from home. We look at the lanterns and then we watch the light show.

I'm still too excited to sleep when we get home so we stay up and put on our own **INK** talent show. Dad does a dance - it's not as good as the dancers who spun on their heads and did flips and tricks, but it's still very funny to watch! Mum tells some cheesy jokes and Granny Gail sings another song. I do some more magic tricks - with the help of Fuzzy, of course.

"One day, Fuzzy," I say. "We can be famous magicians, up on a big stage with our names in lights.

THE GREAT INKTASTIC DESTINY INK and THE MAGNIFICENT FUZZY!"

Fuzzy and I take our biggest bow ever!

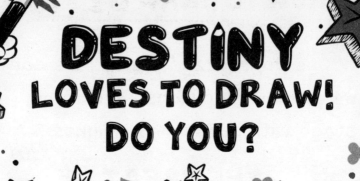

DESTINY
LOVES TO DRAW!
DO YOU?

Here are some
HOW TO DRAW pages for
your favourite characters
from **Talent Show Magic**.
Just grab a pencil and some
paper and copy the lines
given for you.

HAVE FUN!

HOW TO DRAW DESTINY

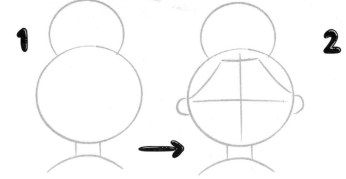

HOW TO DRAW FUZZY

HOW TO DRAW
GRANNY GAIL

LOOK OUT FOR

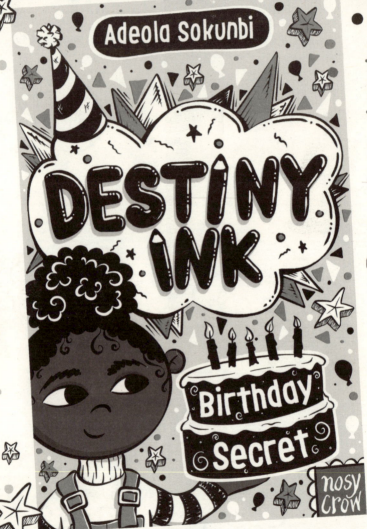

Adeola Sokunbi

DESTINY INK

Birthday Secret

nosy crow

COMING SOON!